SAUSAGES

Jessica Souhami

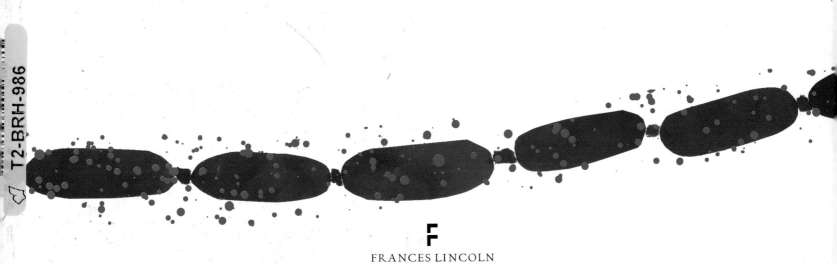

F

FRANCES LINCOLN
CHILDREN'S BOOKS

Sausages is Jessica Souhami's version of a famous story called **The Three Wishes** which can be traced back to Ancient India and Ancient Greece. The first popular version was published in France in the 17th century, but a little-known version from 12th-century Britain also exists. The story most of us know derives from the tale collected by the Grimm brothers in the 19th century.

Sausages copyright © Frances Lincoln Limited 2006
Text and illustrations copyright © Jessica Souhami 2006

First published in Great Britain and the USA in 2006
by Frances Lincoln Children's Books,
4 Torriano Mews, Torriano Avenue, London NW5 2RZ
www.franceslincoln.com

Distributed in the USA by Publishers Group West

British Library Cataloguing in Publication Data available on request

ISBN 978-1-84507-397-8

Illustrated with collage of Ingres paper hand-painted with water colour inks and graphite pencil

Set in HelveticaNeue

Printed in China

9 8 7 6 5 4 3 2

One day, a poor woodcutter called John found an elf stuck on a rose thorn.

"Poor little thing!" said John, and gently lifted the elf free.

"Thank you," said the elf. "In return for your kindness,
I grant you three magic wishes."
He shook out his wings and flew away, calling back,
"Be careful what you wish for!"

And he was gone.

John rushed home to tell his wife the good news.

"Dear Martha," he said, "we shall be rich for the rest of our lives. We must sit down, think hard, and choose our three wishes very carefully."

So John and Martha sat by the fire
and thought and thought, and thought again,
of all the lovely things they could wish for.

But it was difficult to choose.
They sighed, and thought some more.

After several hours, John felt his tummy rumbling.
It would not stop.

"I'm starving, Martha," he said.
"I wish we had some sausages."

And...

...with a **WH...OOO...SH,**
out from the chimney shot a string of sizzling, succulent sausages!

Martha and John stared at the sausages –

and they stared at each other.

"You foolish man!" cried Martha.
"You've wasted a whole wish.

Just think of all the grand things
we could have chosen with that wish.

And all we've got is sausages!

I wish these silly sausages were stuck
to the end of your nose!"

And guess what ...?

The sausages leapt on to the end of John's nose, where they stuck fast.

Two wishes gone and nothing but sausages. And they were on John's nose!

Now John was angry.

"For goodness' sake, Martha," he cried,
"get these things off my nose!"

and she

pulled...

and she tugged...

but she could not pull the sausages

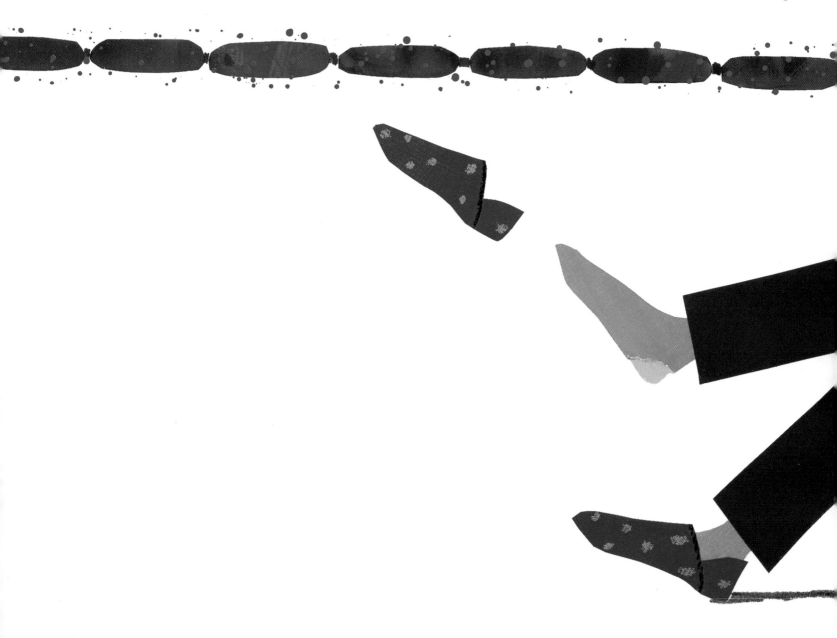

off the end of John's nose.

So she let go and...

John fell on the floor with a bump.

"Oh, by poor, poor dose," he said. "Id's so sore!"

"My dear husband," cried Martha, feeling sorry for John.
"We've been through good times and bad times together.
It's silly for stupid wishes to make us cross."

She took a deep breath.
"I wish these sausages would fall off John's nose."

^{And} **WH...OOOO**

OO....SH, they did.

John gave Martha a big hug.
"Well, my dear, we've lost our chance to be rich.

But we have each other – and a very good dinner!"

And far away, a little elf laughed.